SOPHIA

The Alchemist's Dog

SHELLEY JACKSON

A Richard Jackson Book
Atheneum Books for Young Readers
New York London Toronto Sydney Singapore

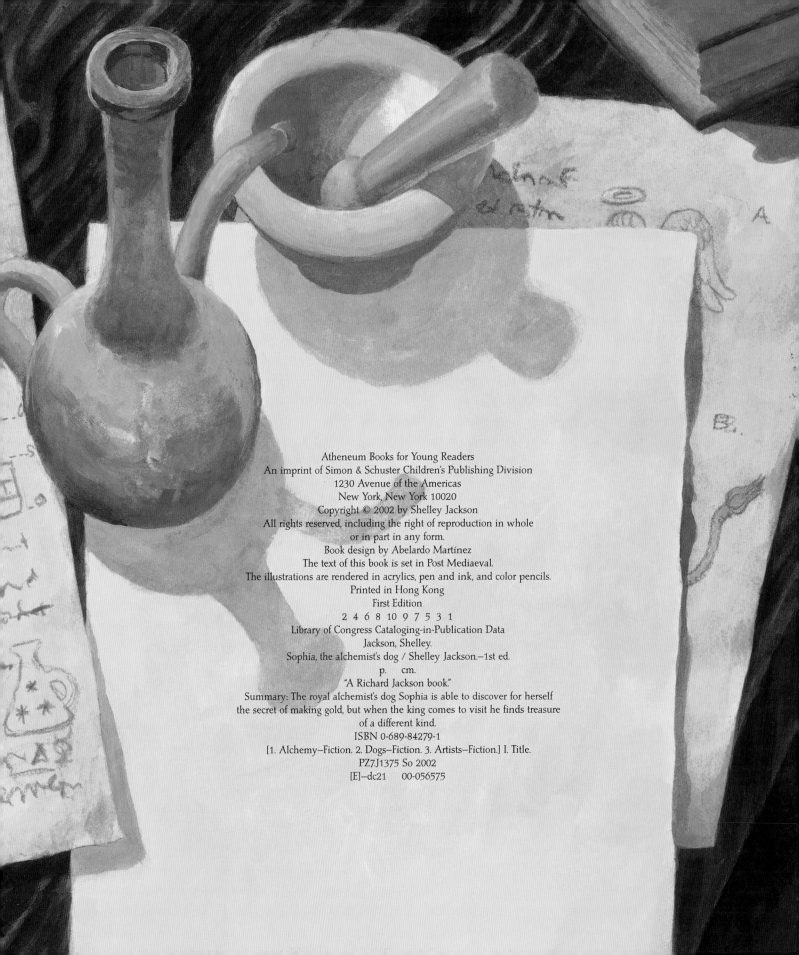

Atheneum Books for Young Readers
An imprint of Simon & Schuster Children's Publishing Division
1230 Avenue of the Americas
New York, New York 10020
Copyright © 2002 by Shelley Jackson
Book design by Abelardo Martínez
The text of this book is set in Post Mediaeval.
The illustrations are rendered in acrylics, pen and ink, and color pencils.
Printed in Hong Kong
First Edition
2 4 6 8 10 9 7 5 3 1
Library of Congress Cataloging-in-Publication Data
Jackson, Shelley.
Sophia, the alchemist's dog / Shelley Jackson.—1st ed.
p.   cm.
"A Richard Jackson book."
Summary: The royal alchemist's dog Sophia is able to discover for herself
the secret of making gold, but when the king comes to visit he finds treasure
of a different kind.
ISBN 0-689-84279-1
[1. Alchemy–Fiction. 2. Dogs–Fiction. 3. Artists–Fiction.] I. Title.
PZ7.J1375 So 2002
[E]–dc21   00-056575

Sophia's master was alchemist to the king, and Sophia thought he was marvelous. He understood many things other humans were too foolish to see, such as the wisdom to be gained by rootling under bushes or inspecting small, creeping things. He knew when Sophia was hungry and when she wanted to go out; in sum, he was almost unbelievably intelligent. But lately her master had not been himself. He was worried. And so was Sophia.

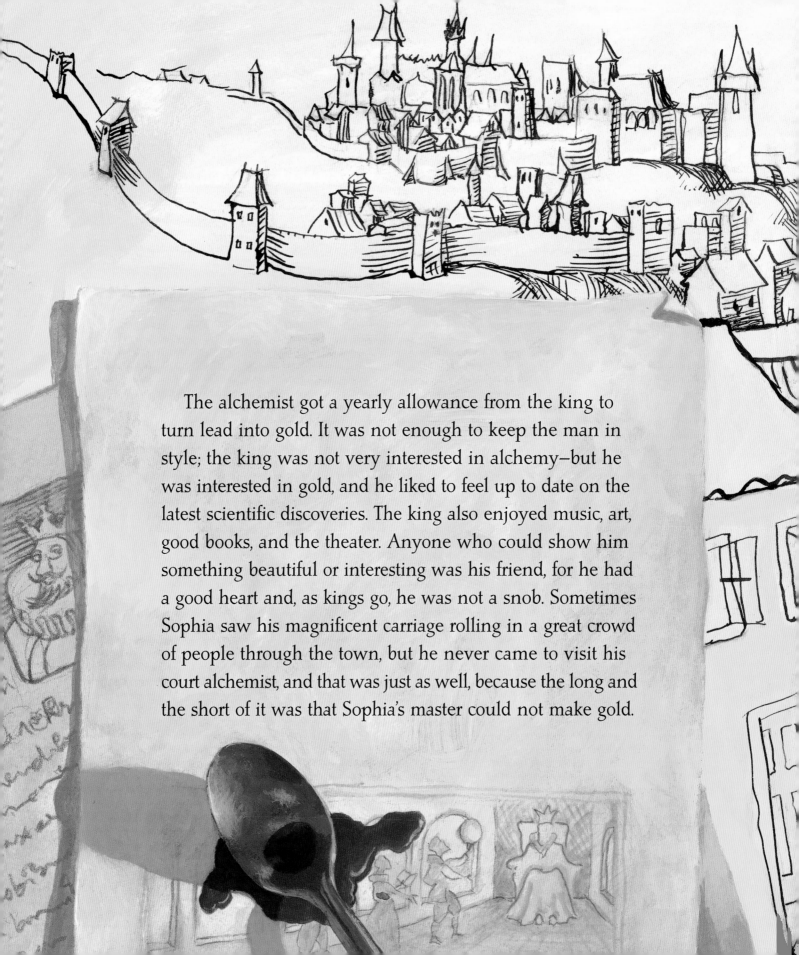

The alchemist got a yearly allowance from the king to turn lead into gold. It was not enough to keep the man in style; the king was not very interested in alchemy—but he was interested in gold, and he liked to feel up to date on the latest scientific discoveries. The king also enjoyed music, art, good books, and the theater. Anyone who could show him something beautiful or interesting was his friend, for he had a good heart and, as kings go, he was not a snob. Sometimes Sophia saw his magnificent carriage rolling in a great crowd of people through the town, but he never came to visit his court alchemist, and that was just as well, because the long and the short of it was that Sophia's master could not make gold.

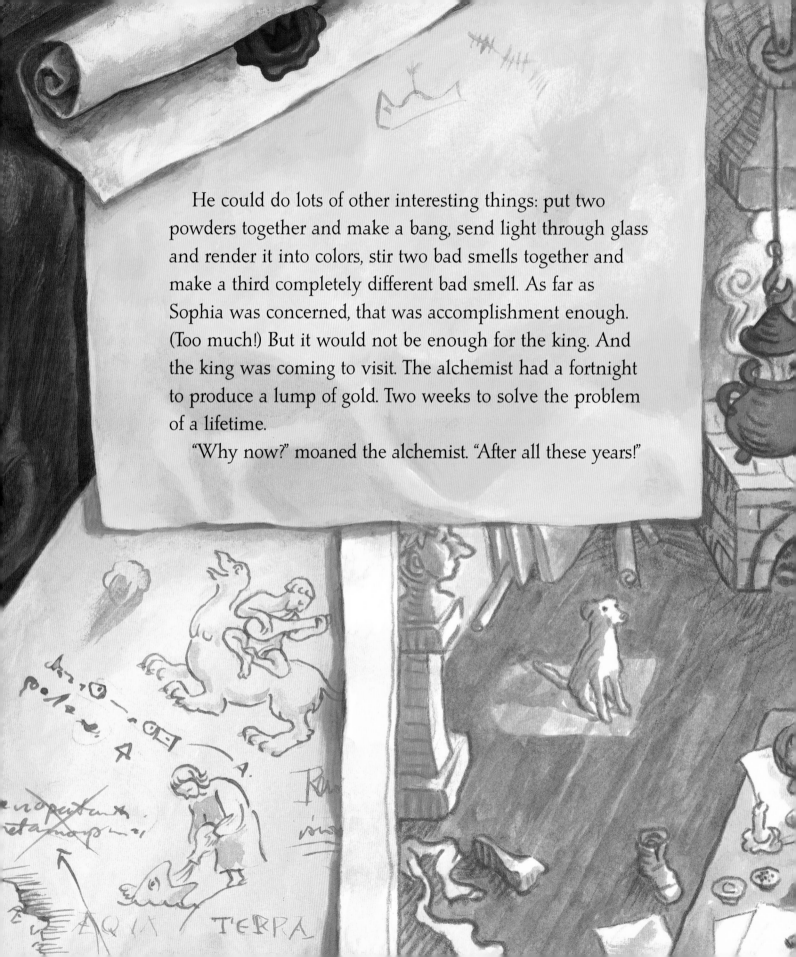

He could do lots of other interesting things: put two powders together and make a bang, send light through glass and render it into colors, stir two bad smells together and make a third completely different bad smell. As far as Sophia was concerned, that was accomplishment enough. (Too much!) But it would not be enough for the king. And the king was coming to visit. The alchemist had a fortnight to produce a lump of gold. Two weeks to solve the problem of a lifetime.

"Why now?" moaned the alchemist. "After all these years!"

Since the word came, the alchemist had not spent one
peaceful night. He heaved and creaked in the crooked bed
with its legs all straining sideways. Sophia set her forepaws
on the mattress and stood up to look at him. His face shone,
greased with sleep. It was fat and congested, wrestling with
invisible things. The quilt flounced as if something more
than human were astir under it, perhaps an imp, and
Sophia stuck her little nose under the blanket, scrabbled
with her hind feet, then tunneled in, neat as a stoat.

She popped up here for air, she popped up there to set a stern eye on the sputtering candle, but she caught nothing this time, though once before she had come up with a smallish imp struggling in her teeth like a rat. She had nudged it firmly through the crack in the door, and guarded the hole until morning, though the taste of sulfur in her mouth made her bare her teeth.

Once, too, she caught an angel, which flared and fizzed in her mouth and half blinded her. Her muzzle had been numb a whole day. She had been embarrassed, but she had not backed down. "No one is allowed to disturb my master's sleep," she said, and she showed the angel the door as well, though she paid it this respect: She allowed it to creep out on its own. The sides of the cracks still glowed in the dark, for some of the angel's shine had rubbed off, like butterfly scales.

But this time only dreams disturbed her master's sleep. "The green lion," he muttered, "the red dove."

What about the brown dog? thought Sophia, climbing off the bed. She turned a few times, then dropped with a groan onto her blanket.

The master had never been afraid of bad dreams. In fact, he believed his dreams, good or bad, held clues to the formulæ he sought. They were like letters in a secret alphabet! Every morning he leaped out of bed and drew foxes, eagles, bodies climbing out of graves, kings swimming with their crowns on their heads, animals that were half rooster, half snake, which made Sophia's fur bristle. He drew everything he had seen in his sleep. Then he hurried to his books and leafed through them, trying to decipher his drawings. "The fox—that's sulfur—and it's running with a burning brand in its mouth—that must mean I am to heat the vessel—and the eagle with two heads—that's—" And it was off to the mortar and pestle, the retorts and alembics, bang and fizzle, and the room full of smoke.

When he had made the room uninhabitable, he whistled
to Sophia and they went out to look for signs and secrets.
Sophia danced ahead, nosing out signs in every tuft of grass
and leaving some of her own. The master, too, found signs
everywhere: the bright zip of light along a length of spider
silk, like a needle flashing across the sky. The thick squiggle
of a snake, startled into a living stripe. The tracks of water
bugs on pond scum. "It's the handwriting of the universe,
Sophia! We just can't read it yet!" he'd say, and set up his
paint box by the pond to copy it down.

Sophia loved their walks. But lately he had neglected to invite her. He would stay out for hours and come home red-eyed and smelling of old manuscripts; he was prowling libraries and bookshops, hunting recipes for gold. At home, his worktable was crowded with bottles of smoke and swirling colors. He scribbled notes and numbers on page after page and when he had filled each page, he dropped it on the floor. The angel and the imp came back, bold as brass—though they treated Sophia with great respect, for they had not forgotten being shown the door—and they often sat on the alchemist's shoulders while he worked. And though he still reached for his pen the moment he woke up, propping his board against the bedclothes and scratching away till his nightcap shook, she saw that he no longer took any joy in it.

A friend came to visit. He looked at the alchemist's papers, piles and piles of them. "Your formulæ don't work," the friend said firmly. "Fire yields nothing but ashes; moistened ashes remain ashes, only damper. You burn expensive chemicals and produce nothing but bad smells. Give it up, for the love of God!"

"I can't! I am on the verge of deciphering, I do not say the heavens, but . . ." He looked at his friend. "No, you don't believe me. But I see visions! Look!" He unrolled scroll after scroll, lifted canvas after canvas from the stack.

The friend looked at them a long time. "Maybe you do see visions," he said, "but kings and courtiers are simple people, and they will want proof that your formulæ work. Do you have proof?"

The alchemist just groaned.

Time was running out. The terrible day was less than a week away. Worry made Sophia careless. She walked absentmindedly through some spilled ink, and when she looked back, there were tracks meandering across a page of his notations.

"Sophia!" exclaimed the master. She went and hid under the bed.

He caught up the page. She peeped out. The master did not seem angry. His face was close to the paper. "This may be the answer! This symbol, here"—he stumbled over and flapped the page in her face—"is it *mercurius vulgaris* or *mercurius philosophicus?*"

She drew back. She didn't know.

"Never mind, never mind!" He bore the sheet away to the table.

Sophia dropped her head onto her blanket. She did not think her paw prints would show him how to make gold.

He spent all day hunched over the marks, turning the paper around and around. When the room grew dark and cold, he moved from the table to the bed and worked on. But at last, when only a finger-joint of candle was left, he threw his pen across the room. The alchemist buried his head into the pillow and wept.

Sophia tried to remind him that there were other things that mattered. Her walks, for example. But he only shook his head. Nothing but gold would make him happy. "Well then," said Sophia to herself, "it is time for me to make some experiments of my own." She knew what to do; she had watched her master often enough. After he had gone to sleep, she set up her own laboratory under the table. She swept up small piles of colored powders with her tail. She carefully lifted glass beakers between her teeth. She fetched burning wood from the fire, water from the bucket by the washstand. She pressed the angel and the imp into service. "You might as well make yourselves useful," she said. They stirred and measured and poured liquids from beaker to beaker, things that were hard for a dog to do.

All night while the master tossed and turned, strange lights and smells came from under the table, but he never woke. Days, Sophia slept curled on her blanket, and the master did not disturb her, for he never went out now. Just sat at his table, leafing listlessly through his books. When Sophia scratched at the door, he opened it but she went out alone and came back when she pleased, because he forgot to call for her. He would have forgotten to let her in again, too, if she didn't bark to remind him.

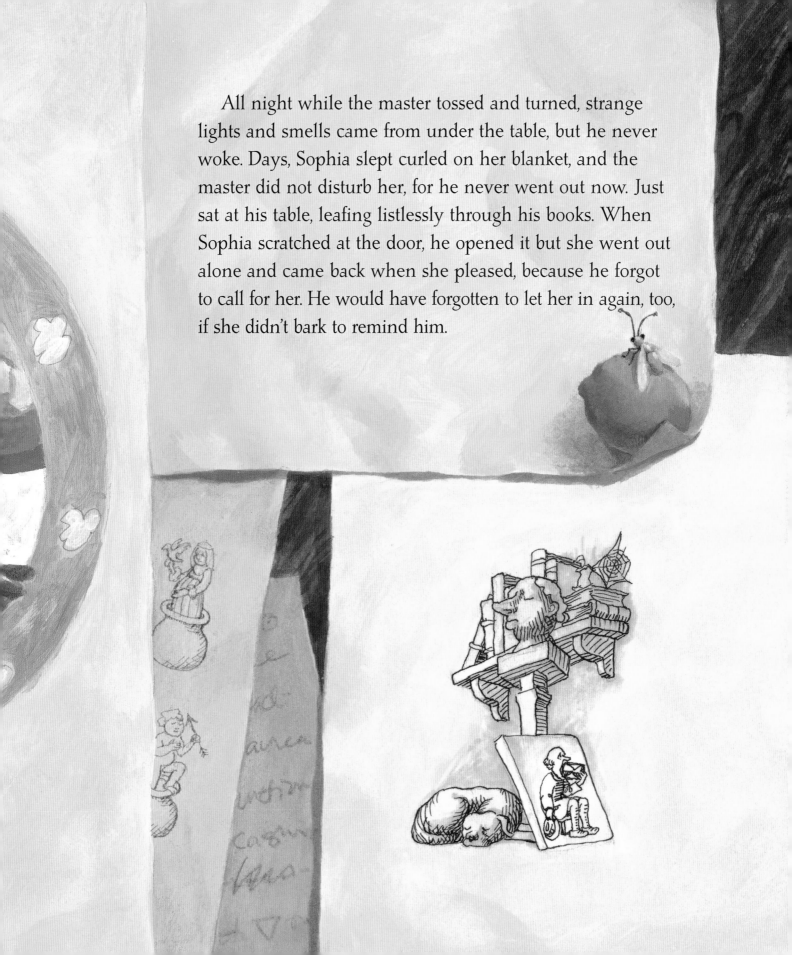

She had only three more nights to save her master. On the first night, Sophia had no better luck than he had had. The poisonous syrups seethed until dawn and left nothing but black gunk behind. The second night was the same story. On the third night, she began to wonder if she was going about it the wrong way.

To clear her mind, she went for a stroll around the little house, nosing through jumbled books, heels of bread, and lost stockings. The master woofed in his dream and fought his pillow, and a piece of paper slid out from under it and danced in the air. It sank down at Sophia's feet.

It was the page of her paw prints. She looked at it sideways and upside down, but it did not look like writing to her. But then, she could not read.

Instead, she put her nose to the page. She smelled fish oil and sage from a dinner four nights ago. She had crunched up the tail: delicious! She smelled smoke and old rags and her master's sweat and her own doggy aroma. Linseed oil, cloves, sulfur, tea. And ink, of course.

Could the philosopher's stone be made of ink? And a pinch of dog hair? Maybe not, but it was a place to start. Cloves, paper, a drop of sweat. She was not an alchemist, she was a dog. A dog must follow her nose.

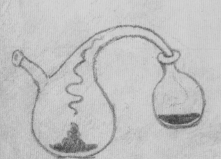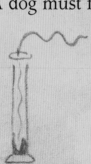

That night, after many stinks had arisen from her laboratory under the table, a beaker cracked and fell open like a tulip. In its shards lay a knob of shining metal.

At last she had made something happen!

Sophia pawed it out of the broken glass and looked closely at it. She pushed it with her nose. It was very heavy. Sophia let out a stifled woof and then rolled on the gold, kicking her feet in the air.

The angel and the imp walked up and stared at her. "You are a strange being," said the angel. "What are you doing?"

Sophia sat up. "It's a thing dogs do," she said, "to celebrate."

With dignity, though she couldn't stop her tail from wagging, she trotted to her blanket. She curled up delightedly and flopped her tail over her eyes.

The imp and the angel were still looking at her. Sophia shifted her tail and opened one eye. "Go to bed," she said. "Our work's done." With a deep sigh of satisfaction, she fell asleep.

The next morning the king was due and the alchemist did not want to get up. He flinched at every sound from the street: Was it the king? He sat hunched on his bed, wrapped in his blanket, until Sophia brought his clothes and sat over them with a very stern expression on her face.

"You are very demanding," he told her. "There is no point in getting dressed—or indeed in doing anything at all—but I will, for you."

Well before the king arrived, Sophia heard the clopping of hoofs on cobblestones. She was peering out the window when he stepped out of the carriage. He was a small man, but very well-dressed. He swept into the room into the center of a crowd of fine ladies and gentlemen, and Sophia hid under the table. The king was loud. His courtiers were louder, and very silly. The king's astrologer styled himself an expert on alchemy as well, and was there to offer his opinion. Sophia did not like him.

"You may be a fair philosopher," the astrologer said to her master, "though I doubt it, but you are certainly no alchemist. Have you produced any gold at all? A grain?"

The alchemist frowned and took an angry sip of his cold tea. The courtiers simpered and curtsied meaninglessly to one another. The king looked embarrassed, because he was kind.

Under the table, Sophia sat ready beside the lump of gold. She would make sure the king got what he came for. The angel and the imp sat nearby, waiting and watching.

"Go on," said the imp, giggling. "Make a fool of them all! Roll it right into the middle of the room! I'll help!" He rushed forward, but Sophia snarled and he stopped in his tracks.

"I see no reason to stay here a moment longer," the astrologer said, wiping his nose fastidiously.

Sophia set her muzzle behind the nugget, and was about to give it a push when the king cleared his throat rather loudly. "But I see a reason," he said.

Sophia peered out from under the table. The king held something in his hand, one of the alchemist's sketches. "Do you have more of these?" he asked.

"Everywhere," the alchemist said, waving his hand vaguely about. "I see visions, but they are deceitful. I have long sought the secret meanings of the universe in their portents. But the formulæ are not concealed in them. I have been misled, and I have wasted Your Majesty's time. The astrologer is right: I have not made even a grain of gold."

Under the table, Sophia growled to hear her master speak so humbly.

"Formulæ?" said the king. "Perhaps not. But treasure? Enough to fill a vault!"

"Where? Where?" The courtiers whiffled, gathering around. Puzzled, Sophia came out from under the table.

The king propped a canvas up against the wall and stepped back to look at it. He laughed and clapped the alchemist on both shoulders at once. "You are no longer the alchemist to the king," he announced.

The alchemist hung his head.

"Instead," said the king grandly, for he enjoyed a dramatic moment as much as anyone, "you are painter to the king. Yes, you shall paint for me. The whole world will know your name—but everyone will call you Master—or Maestro, after the Italian manner—for that is what you are!" The courtiers clapped politely, the astrologist sneezed, and the master sank down on his bed in bewilderment, but Sophia stood up proudly and wagged her tail.

The gold was forgotten under the table. A few busy days later, Sophia came across it. She considered it for a while, her paw raised. Then she pushed it down a mouse hole.

"It's another kind of alchemy," said the painter to his friend, tipping powdered pigment out of a mortar into a bowl of egg yolks. "Naples yellow, ochre, a little lead white . . . lo! Gold!"